No More Poems!

A BOOK IN VERSE THAT JUST GETS WORSE

BY

Rhett Miller

ART BY

Dan Santat

Megan Tingley Books
LITTLE, BROWN AND COMPANY
NEW YORK BOSTON

A NOTE TO THE READER

I hold dear the rules of grammar and punctuation, the sensible guidelines to which we adhere in order to make our communication efficient, effective, and, ultimately, powerful. As is the case with many rules, however, the rules of grammar and punctuation sometimes need to be broken! Silly, subversive poems where the words want to trip over one another? Scattershot dispatches from often unreliable narrators in a mad rush to tell their sketchy story? Late-night, little-kid mind-explosions where the line between dream and reality blurs? In my humble opinion, this book is no place for rules. In real life, however, I ask you to please use your commas wisely and always end your sentences with a period

Rhett Miller

OLD 97's FOREVER

ABOUT THIS BOOK: The illustrations for this book were done in pencil, watercolor, and Adobe Photoshop. This book was edited by Megan Tingley and designed by David Caplan and Nicole Brown. The production was supervised by Erika Schwartz, and the production editor was Jen Graham. The text was set in Archer.

Text copyright © 2019 by Rhett Miller • Illustrations copyright © 2019 by Dan Santat • Cover illustration copyright © 2019 by Dan Santat • Cover design by David Caplan • Cover copyright © 2019 by Hachette Book Group, Inc. • Hachette Book Group supports the right to free expression and the value of copyright. The purpose of copyright is to encourage writers and artists to produce the creative works that enrich our culture. • The scanning, uploading, and distribution of this book without permission is a theft of the author's intellectual property. If you would like permission to use material from the book (other than for review purposes), please contact permissions@hbgusa.com. Thank you for your support of the author's rights. • Little, Brown and Company • Hachette Book Group • 1290 Avenue of the Americas, New York, NY 10104 • Visit us at LBYR.com • First Edition: March 2019 • Little, Brown and Company is a division of Hachette Book Group, Inc. The Little, Brown name and logo are trademarks of Hachette Book Group, Inc. • The publisher is not responsible for websites (or their content) that are not owned by the publisher. • Library of Congress Cataloging-in-Publication Data • Names: Miller, Rhett, author. | Santat, Dan, illustrator. • Title: No more poems! / by Rhett Miller ; with pictures by Dan Santat • Description: First edition. | New York : Little, Brown and Company, 2019. • Identifiers: LCCN 2018017609 | ISBN 9780316416528 (hardcover) | ISBN 9780316416498 (ebook) | ISBN • 9780316416504 (library edition ebook) • Subjects: LCSH: Children's poetry, American. | Humorous poetry. • Classification: LCC PS3613.I5523 A6 2019 | DDC 811/.6—dc23 • LC record available at https://lccn.loc.gov/2018017609 • ISBNs: 978-0-316-41652-8 (hardcover), 978-0-316-41649-8 (ebook), 978-0-316-52406-3 (ebook), 978-0-316-52405-6 (ebook) • PRINTED IN CHINA • 1010 • 10 9 8 7 6 5 4 3 2

For Peteybird and The Mooch, the awesomest twerps in the world —RM

For Alek, Kyle, and Leah —DS

CONTENTS

MY SECRET KARATE

There's a type of karate I specialize in
I invented it all on my own
No one has witnessed my secret karate
It's meant to be practiced alone

I stand on my left foot and raise my right leg
Using muscles in abs, thighs and tush
And with just the toe of my special blue sneaker
I make the toilet flush

I toggle the lever or mash down the button
Or lean on the handle just so
That way my fingertip never gets yucky
Thanks to the skills of my toe

Courtesy's something my mom always taught me
Starting when I was a kid
So using the toe of my special blue sneaker
I lower the seat and the lid

My secret karate is practiced in private
In public bathroom stalls
I don't mean to brag but my balance is awesome
I never touch the walls

I don't have a name for my potty karate
I might call it Tae Kwon Doo
Or maybe I'll say I'm a third degree black belt
In the top secret art of Kung Poo

Purple Pox

I woke up today with Purple Pox
I gotta stay home from school
These purple dots appeared out of nowhere
I'm as surprised as you

Additional symptoms, you ask? I dunno
I guess otherwise I feel fine
But if I show up at school like this
My teacher will lose her mind

The research I've done says treatments include
Candy and video games
Lots and lots of stupid TV
And calling your sister names

I hear Purple Pox doesn't last very long
Right around seven hours
I should be better by 3:25
After a hot, soapy shower

On a totally unrelated note
If you're stopping by the store
My purple markers ran out of ink
I could use a couple more

Brotherly Love

Please don't push your brother
Out the window, Little Miss
I know he's asking for it
I am quite aware of this
But if you push your brother
Out the window he'll go splat
And once he's squished
There isn't any coming back from that

Please don't drown your brother
In the bathtub, Sweetie Pea
He can be a twerp sometimes
I know, believe you me
But if you dunk him three times
And he only comes up two
The cops'll be all over us
There's nothing I can do

If you take a pillow
And you smother brother's head
I've got a strong suspicion
That he just might wake up dead
Or worse he'd be a vegetable
Oh bitter irony
He hasn't eaten one of those
In his whole history

Darling little girl
I know exactly who they'd blame
If you go pouring gasoline
And setting him aflame
You're much too young to shoulder
Such responsibility
I'm the one they'd cart off
To the penitentiary

If you tie your brother
To an active railroad track
I'm the one they'll take away
Never to come back
Feed your brother poison
Maybe drop him down a well
And *I'm* the one who'll wind up
Living in a prison cell

And so I beg you, Honey Pie,
Ignore your dark desires
Maybe give his dirt bike
A couple of flat tires
Or if he's by a swimming pool
Give a gentle shove
But please, my angel, show a little
Brotherly love

MY DEVICE

I used to find it charming
I used to think it nice
But now I am a prisoner
Of my own device

I need it to take pictures
I need it to play games
Remember all my numbers
Remember all my names

It tells me where I'm going
It gives me all my news
It plays me all my music
It buys me all my shoes

I used to go to Mom's house
With a birthday cake
Now I simply text her
Don't even have to bake

I once had conversations
With people that I met
It used to make me nervous
It used to make me sweat

Now I can ignore them
And look down at my screen
They don't even notice
They're doing the same thing

My device is smarter
Than everyone I meet
It knows all the answers
You're all obsolete

hairs

Nose hairs are gross hairs
We all know it's true
Ear hairs are weird hairs
They're pretty gross too
But…
When one long hair grows
From a mole on your nose
Man, I feel sorry for you

WEIR OF THE

Weirdos of the world unite
Stand up and rejoice
Sing your happy weirdo song
Use your big kid voice

I'm a total weirdo
I like doing math
I like reading mysteries
While I'm in the bath

Sister she's a weirdo
Wears different color socks
Grandma she's a weirdo
She has seven cuckoo clocks

Daddy's such a weirdo
That he likes black licorice
Mommy's such a weirdo
She's not even ticklish

DOS WORLD UNITE!

My doctor she's a weirdo
Always dressed up all in white
My teacher is a weirdo
He plays saxophone at night

The guy who drives my school bus
Is particularly weird
The older kids say he has
A bird's nest in his beard

My babysitter keeps a penny
Hidden in her shoe
Her boyfriend still reads comic books
They're both weirdos too

You know who else is weird
Is the librarian from school
I saw her do a backflip
At the local swimming pool

The mayor's unicycle
The crossing guard's kazoo
Suggest that they might both in fact
Be secret weirdos too

I thought we were outnumbered
One thing's becoming clear though
Every single one of us
It turns out, is a weirdo

MY TWIN

I'm not my twin
My twin is my twin
He is who he is
And I am not him

Mom says she loves us
Exactly the same
Which doesn't make sense
He's dumb

He breathes through his mouth
He talks with it full
A mile a minute
With never a lull

He wishes he was
As clever as me
But too bad for him
He's dumb

I was here first
Five minutes before
I'm wiser because
I've seen so much more

He'll never catch up
He'll just tag along
What do you expect?
He's dumb

He built a rocket
Out in the yard
I coulda done it
It isn't that hard

The thing barely made it
Out into orbit
Proving again
He's dumb

Accepted to college
Seven years early
They must be confused
They wanted me surely

I'm not my twin
My twin is my twin
He'd like to be me
But I'm glad I'm not him

It takes a big brain
To be nasty as me
He's always nice
He's dumb

If ignorance is
Really bliss like they say
No wonder I'm miserable
All the dang day

My twin's always happy
And smile-y and laugh-y
I rest my case
He's dumb

An honest mistake
We do look alike
The big difference is
He's dumb

I can do math
Like adding and minuses
His math's all messed up
With x's and y's and stuff

My grammar good
His words be confusing
They must be made up
He's dumb

THIS BATHTUB'S TOO SMALL

This bathtub's too small
Or there's too many kids in it
Everyone stop horsing 'round
For a minute
A blob of shampoo
Landed right in my eye
And a toenail just scratched me
From ankle to thigh
We might be too old
To all wash in one tub
There's no room to soap up
There's no room to scrub
I'm dirtier now
Than before I got in
The cheek I just washed
Wasn't next to a chin
I gotta get out of this
Tub full of troubles
Now someone's making
Mysterious bubbles

I want a dog
Not a pussycat, they're much too shifty
They look like they'd steal all your money
Plus they poop in a box in your house

I want a dog
Not a parakeet, they're way too chirpy
The dang things, they never get sleepy
But a dog and me? We could be pals

I want a dog
I'll walk it and feed it and pet it
If I don't get a dog you'll regret it
That's not a threat, it's just true

I want a dog
Not toys or money or candy
There's no single thing you could hand me
Besides a dang dog that'll do

I want a dog
Not a hamster for Pete's sake—they're stinky
And their eyes are all tiny and blinky
A dog looks right into your soul

I want a dog
A snake? You've got to be kidding
He'd probably do some wizard's bidding
Then slither off into some hole

I want a dog
I'd wash it and groom it and love it
And take such amazing care of it
I know we'd be best friends for sure

I want a dog
The other kids don't understand me
They're all either sportsy or fancy
And none of them have any fur

I want a dog
If you get a fish and you spoil it
You flush the poor guy down the toilet
How is that fun for a kid?

I want a dog
I don't want some boring old bunny
Though buck teeth and big ears *are* funny
But she'll hop away soon as she's fed

I want a dog
I'll give you until my next birthday
If there's no dog by then I am RUNNING AWAY
I'll go off and live in a bog

I WANT A DOG!
A DOG DOG DOG DOG DOG DOG DOG!
I'll be in my room with the door double locked
Until you guys get me A DOG!

My Homework

I did my homework but I lost it
My mom might've thought it was garbage and tossed it
My stupid sister might've hid it
One thing's for certain though, I did it

I remember it took me over an hour
Which left me without even time to shower
If I smell ripe, then that's the reason
And also right now it's basketball season

My dad might've grabbed it to write down a number
As he gets older he *is* getting dumber
How does he manage to hold down a job?
He's ditzy as heck and he's kind of a slob

I guess it's not *all* my family's fault
I *could* keep my homework locked in a vault
With skulls and crossbones and seventeen locks
Under a mountain of stinky old socks

Or handcuff a briefcase onto my wrist
To carry the homework I swear *does* exist
Police motorcade? A squadron of goons?
I should have hired soldiers! Entire platoons!

To bring you my homework…

What's that you say?
We didn't have any work due for today?
Nothing?
For real?
No homework assigned?

Never mind

HOW TO PLAY Baseball

You hang out on a diamond
Wearing pj's and a cap
Sometimes you might catch a ball
And folks politely clap
Sometimes you don't catch a ball
And some folks might get mad
Especially the scary coach
Joe Moroni's dad

He's screaming and he's stomping
Spittle flying from his face
He's kicking up a dust storm
Between home plate and first base
It's like *he* never dropped a ball
Never made an error
The kids all pray for rainouts
'Cause the coach is such a terror

Poor Joe's on the mound right now
He'd quit, but he's no quitter
He tries to sneak a fastball past
The other team's best hitter
The bat emits a *crack-a-lack*
That makes your whole team wince
The ball sails in slow-motion
Far beyond the right-field fence

Coach Moroni points
A stubby finger at his son
"YOU THROW ONE MORE MEATBALL, KID,
AND YOU, MY FRIEND, ARE DONE."
Normally at this point
Poor Joe's eyes well up with crying
Today there's something different though
Joe's eyes are dad-defying

Coach don't seem to notice
But the kids all sense a thrill
Joe don't look so poor no more
Up there on the hill

A mom off in the bleachers whispers,
"What a piece of work."
A dad says, even louder,
"That Moroni's such a jerk."
The ump, a local high school kid
Who's getting quite an earful
Is trying to look tough
But only ends up looking tearful

So here's how you play baseball
With a bully for a coach
You hang out on a diamond
Wishing storm clouds would approach

Poor Joe is a peaceful kid
But *gosh* he looks so tough
He winds up and delivers
His most heavy-duty stuff

Joe Moroni sends one flying
Toward his old man's head
Turns out it's a curveball
And it hits the dirt instead

Eyes as big as baseballs
Coach is staring at his son
Joe yells, "Lighten up, Dad,
Us kids wanna have some fun!"

Sun comes out
The coach sits down
His face is kinda gray
We all pound our mitts and smile
We've got a game to play

STINKY-MOUTH YOU

Don't brush your teeth on a rock-and-roll tour
Your mouth should smell worse than a big-city sewer
Your teeth should grow moss and your tongue should grow grass
And your tonsils should slowly grow bluer and bluer

There's eight of you stuck in a six-person van
Although if you follow my yucky-mouth plan
You might even get your own bench in the back
Just make your mouth smell like an old garbage can

Gargle with garlic
Floss with old socks
Rinse with ranch dressing, repeat
You're building a smell
That's designed to repel
Out of all the gross stuff that you eat

You might pay a price when the rock tour is through
Your band might do what bands have been known to do
Break up and start over the very next day
But this time they won't invite
STINKY-MOUTH YOU

TIME † WRESTLE

Time to wrestle
Time to wrestle
Grab yourself a corner of the bed
Jump up and down
But not too high
The ceiling fan will hit you in the head

Time to wrestle
Time to wrestle
Everybody pile on Dad
Nobody jump on
Sweet little sister
You don't wanna see her when she's mad

Time to wrestle
Time to wrestle
Everybody got a second wind
Mama mighta said
It's time for bed
But we all know it's time for WRESTLIN'

DISCO BATH

Disco bath party
Grab a disco ball
Turn off all the other lights
And *wocka wocka wocka wocka wah*

Disco bath party
Disco lights flash
If you got no disco ball
Just flick the switch real fast
Make a lotta bubbles
Use bubble bath or else
Eat some beans for dinner
Make some bubbles for yourself

Disco bath party
Grab a disco ball
Turn off all the other lights
And *wocka wocka wocka wocka wah*

Disco bath party
Got it goin' on
Point your finger at the sky
And sing a disco song
Make a lotta ruckus
Get water on the floor
Ignore your daddy when he says
"DON'T DISCO ANYMORE."

Disco bath party
Grab a disco ball
Turn off all the other lights
And *wocka wocka wocka wocka wah*

How long should we stay here?
At least a half an hour!
When we get out of the bath?
Party in the shower!

Disco ain't for old folks
Disco's for the young
Until the young get sleepy
Then the disco party's done

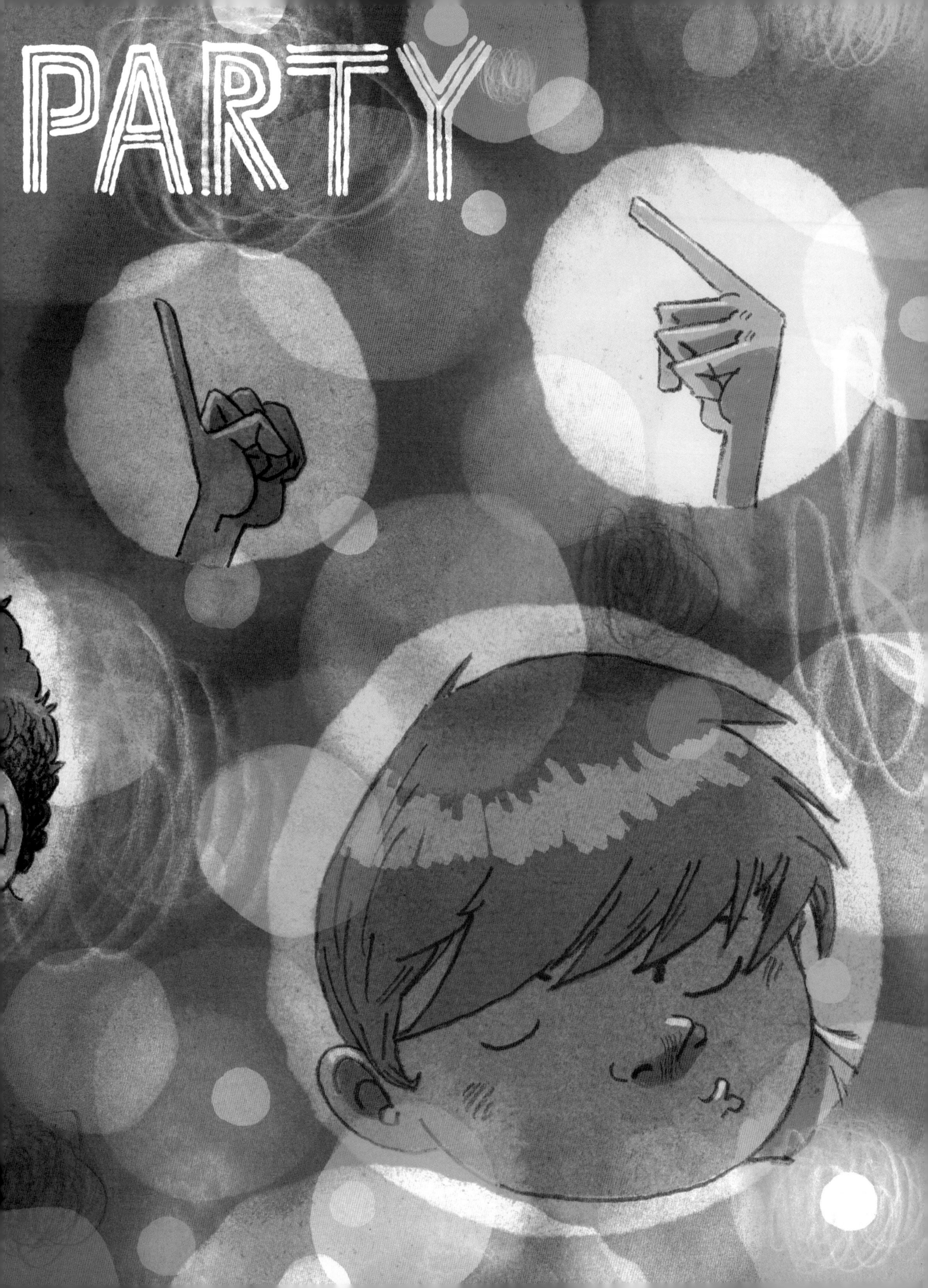
PARTY

i will not go to bed.

I will not go to bed
It's only 10:03
I don't have to do what you say
You're not the boss of me

I will not go to bed
It's only 10:38
I'm almost twelve years old
And it's barely even late

I will not go to bed
It's only 11:02
I'm not even tired yet
And there's so many things to do

I will not go to bed
It's only 11:04
Stop ordering me around
I'm not a baby any...
SNORE...

3:00 AM PEE

I woke up at three
I had to go pee
The house was dark and still
But I was too scared
To go it alone
So I got Bumblebee Bill

Bill isn't mean
His stinger can't sting
He's little and fuzzy and sweet
So I grabbed Yoshi
A panda who's squishy
But cranky when he doesn't eat

Oswald's a puppy
He's floppy and fluffy
I thought he could come along too
He's not very scary
He's mostly just hairy
With eyes that are great big and blue

Dolly's a blankey
She's velvet and swanky
And totally not very tough
I figured, why not?
I'll take all that I got
So I gathered my stuffies all up

James the Rhinoceros
Todd the Koala
A teddy bear named Annie Lee
What we lacked in fearsome
We made up for in numbers
And man I sure did have to pee

MY MANNERS

I drink my soda pop and burp
My manners are a mess
I never say YES MA'AM or SIR
I say UH-HUH or YES
When someone asks
Would I want something
I don't think I would
I never say NO THANK YOU
Instead I say I'M GOOD
But am I?
Really?
Am I good?
In some ways
SURE?
I GUESS?
But one thing's undeniable
My manners are A MESS

I'M NOT HUNGRY ANYMORE

This fish is my dinner
He's looking at me
It's freaking me out
Can the poor guy still see?
I bet I no longer
Look hungry to him
He used to chase tadpoles
And aimlessly swim
Now he's well-done,
Wide-eyed on a plate
We both learned our lesson
A tad bit too late

Before you chomp down
As that minnow swims past
Make sure there's no hook
Or it might be your last
And me, I now know
One thing I must do
Pay closer attention
When reading the menu

HELLO MY NAME IS
Forgive me, I can't quite remember your name
My memory ain't what it was
You look like you're prob'ly a really cool dude
I'm guessing your name may be…Buzz?
That's just a guess! I'm just feeling it out
Is it Bob? Bobby? Maybe Bam Bam?
No. Wait! Don't tell me
It's some sort of title—
Yancy Who Smells Like a Yam?

Why are you getting So bent out of shape? That still isn't my *final* guess I'm sounding it out Just gimme a minute I'm sure I know just what it is
Harry? Stinky? Popeye? Mortimer? Lester the Loogie Machine? Pinhead? Firefly? Knock-Kneed Nathaniel? Mikey the Magical Bean?
I can't help but think When I look at you You've got a name that's a little bit gross Billy Joe Blah Blah the Big Booger Eater? Am I *even getting close*?
Fine. Just tell me Though I guarantee It's the next one that I would have said
No flippin' way You've got to be kidding What kind of freak is named Fred?

ROCK STAR DAD

My dad is a rock star
And I'm just like whatever
Don't ask him if he'll play for you
'Cause he'll go on forever
He's got a lot of fans and stuff
But me, I am not one
I am his thirteen-year-old
Uninterested son

One guy at the show
Got so worked up I thought he'd cry
I'm like are you kidding?
My dad's such a boring guy
I guess I like his scrambled eggs
He gives a mean foot rub
But why must these fanatics
Pack themselves into the club?

At home he's just a goofball
In his saggy pj pants
I can't believe they actually pay
To see him dance
He lays 'round watching football
In a sweatshirt and a cap
He drools like a hound dog
Every time he takes a nap

He's singing in the kitchen
He's singing in the car
I swear my dad is singing
Almost everywhere we are
I hear him all the time
He is a singing fool, my pop
I'm saving up my money
Just to pay my dad *to stop*

I miss the old man
When he's out on tour
I can't deny it
I miss his dorky dad jokes
And the house is way too quiet

Me, I'm no fanatic
But I guess he's not so bad
To me he's not a rock star
He's a *rock star dad*

Way up on the mountain
There's a hairy little man
And if you want a question answered
He's the one who can

You start up in the morning
And you climb all afternoon
And by the time you reach his cave
The only light's the moon

You think that he'd be lonely
But really he's a grump
His fingers grip a walking stick
His back is one big hump

He croaks, "You get one question.
You better ask it quick."
And suddenly you have to pee
Your tummy's feeling sick

You're sure you had a question
You thought about all day
But now your tongue's all big and dry
You don't know what to say

Your mouth is stuck wide-open
Your lips move up and down
You're making all these crazy faces
You can't make a sound

Your belly gives a rumble
Your bladder's feeling full
Where you used to have a brain
Your head is stuffed with wool

THE WISE MAN

The old man lifts an eyebrow
His face a furry mask
And cups his hand behind his ear
To hear what you might ask

The hairy fellow says,
"One question, kid, don't spoil it."
You hear your voice come squeaking out
"May I please use your toilet?"

MY POMES

I am a man
Who is paid to write pomes
Artists like me
Don't need regular homes
We live in the clouds
With our heads full of words
Not down in the dirt
With all of you nerds

My pomes are the gift
I give to mankind
My pomes are the purpose
For which I'm designed
My pomes are so brilliant
They light up the earth
So what do you think
Pomes that awesome are worth?

I'd say for starters
A million or two
Maybe a trillion
Before I'm all through
I should be richer
Than rock stars and kings!
The fact that I'm not?
Well, frankly, it stings

You know what?
Forget it
It stinks being poor
I'm not gonna write y'all no pomes anymore

NO MORE POEMS

No more daylight, it's all gone
No more goofy little songs
Time to put your pj's on
No more poems

No more wrestlin' on the rug
Brush your teeth and one more hug
Tuck you in all nice and snug
No more poems

Time for all the sleepyheads
To climb into their comfy beds
Lights turned out and *goodnight*s said
No more poems

Tomorrow is another day
You'll have silly things to say
We'll have games that we can play
But now the time has slipped away
I'm really sorry, kid, but hey

No

More

Poems!